Numeralia

A POEM BY
JORGE LUJÁN

ILLUSTRATED BY
ISOL

TRANSLATED BY SUSAN OURIOU

- 6 - 7 - 8 - 9 - 10

GROUNDWOOD BOOKS   HOUSE OF ANANSI PRESS   TORONTO BERKELEY

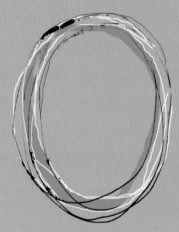

for the way an egg stands

1 for the world's smallest flag

 for the duckling who is not so ugly after all

3 for bedtime kisses when night falls

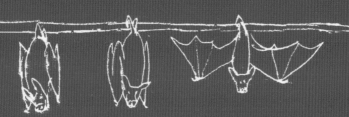

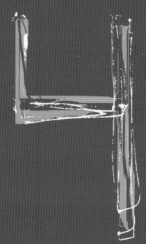 for a chair hanging by its legs

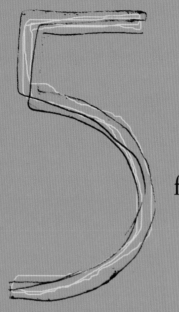 for secret creatures in a glove

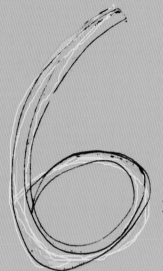 for musketeers alongside their reflection

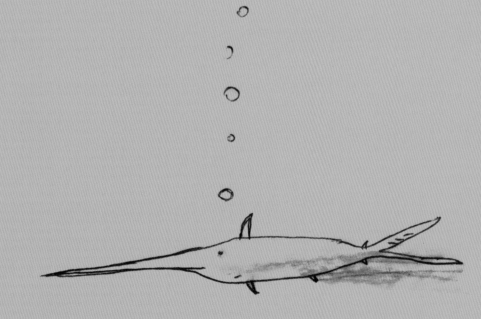

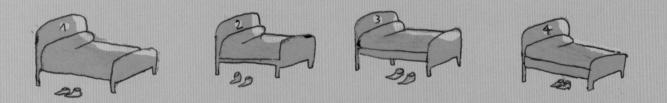

7 for Snow White's friendly dwarfs

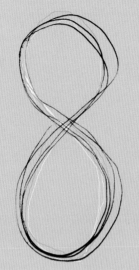

for sand counting out the hours

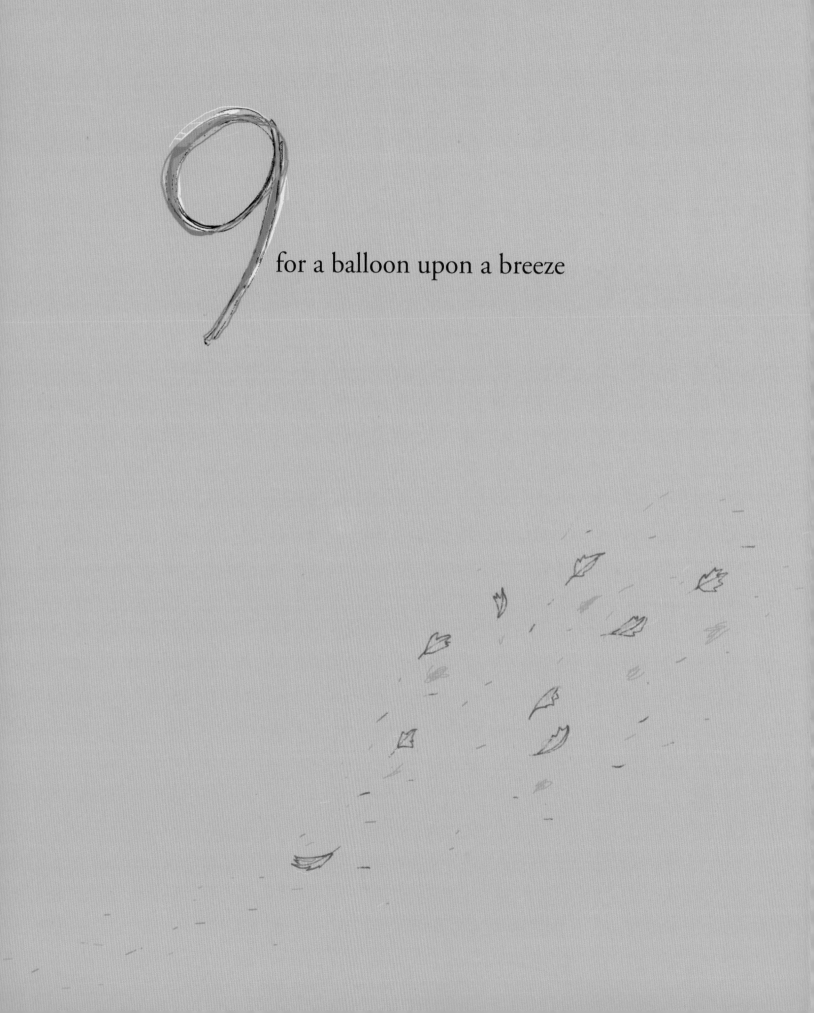

9 for a balloon upon a breeze

10

for a student's thoughts
lost in daydreams

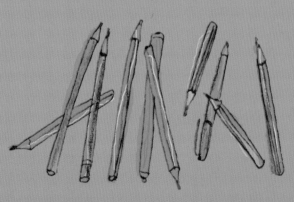

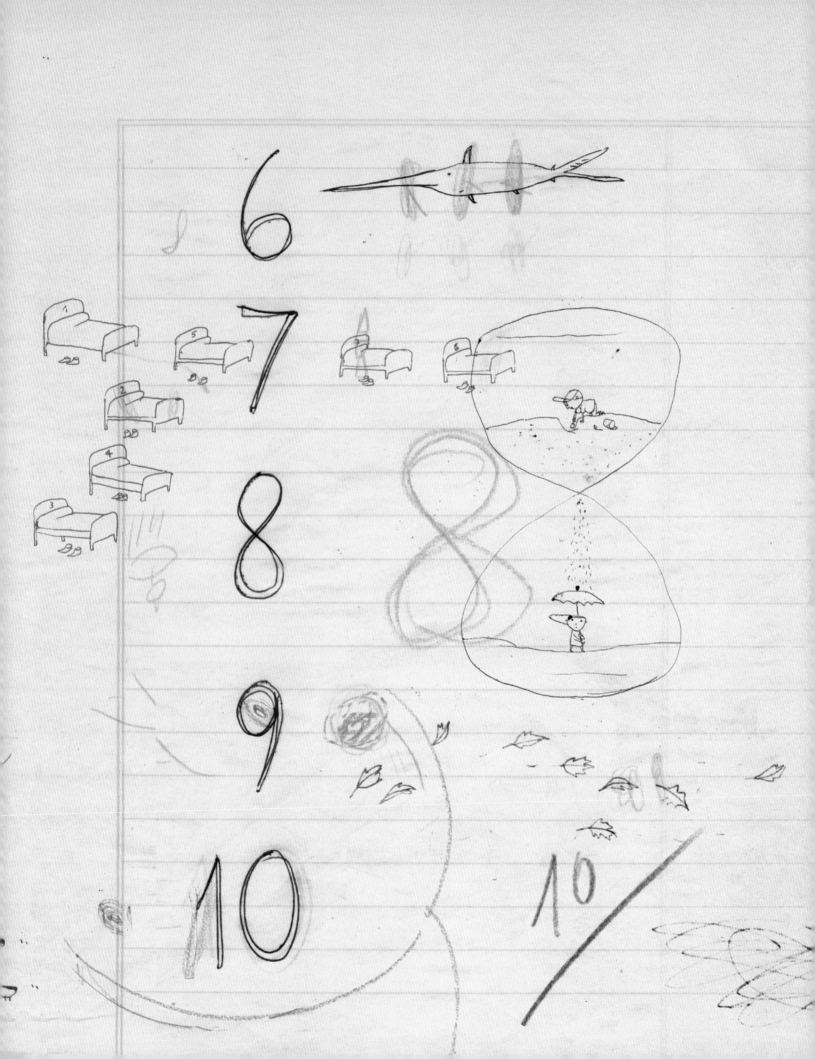